Dear Parent:

Congratulations! Your child is taking the first steps on an exciting journey. The destination? Independent reading!

STEP INTO READING® will help your child get there. The program offers five steps to reading success. Each step includes fun stories and colorful art. There are also Step into Reading Sticker Books, Step into Reading Math Readers, Step into Reading Phonics Readers, Step into Reading Write-In Readers, and Step into Reading Phonics Boxed Sets—a complete literacy program with something for every child.

Learning to Read, Step by Step!

Ready to Read   Preschool–Kindergarten
• big type and easy words • rhyme and rhythm • picture clues
For children who know the alphabet and are eager to begin reading.

Reading with Help   Preschool–Grade 1
• basic vocabulary • short sentences • simple stories
For children who recognize familiar words and sound out new words with help.

Reading on Your Own   Grades 1–3
• engaging characters • easy-to-follow plots • popular topics
For children who are ready to read on their own.

Reading Paragraphs   Grades 2–3
• challenging vocabulary • short paragraphs • exciting stories
For newly independent readers who read simple sentences with confidence.

Ready for Chapters   Grades 2–4
• chapters • longer paragraphs • full-color art
For children who want to take the plunge into chapter books but still like colorful pictures.

STEP INTO READING® is designed to give every child a successful reading experience. The grade levels are only guides. Children can progress through the steps at their own speed, developing confidence in their reading, no matter what their grade.

Remember, a lifetime love of reading starts with a single step!

Step into Reading, Random House, and the Random House colophon are registered trademarks of Random House, Inc.

Visit us on the Web!
StepIntoReading.com
SesameStreetBooks.com
randomhouse.com/kids
www.sesamestreet.org

Educators and librarians, for a variety of teaching tools, visit us at RHTeachersLibrarians.com

Library of Congress Cataloging-in-Publication Data
Ross, Katharine. Elmo and Grover, come on over! / by Katharine Ross.
    p. cm. — (Step into Reading. A step 1 book)
Summary: With the help of friends, Elmo and Grover make a kite.
ISBN 978-0-449-81065-1 (trade) — ISBN 978-0-375-97148-8 (lib. bdg.) — ISBN 978-0-307-97987-2 (ebook)
[1. Kites—Fiction. 2. Puppets—Fiction.] I. Title. II. Series: Step into reading. Step 1 book.
PZ7.R719693Gr 1991 [E]—dc20 90-33947 CIP AC

Printed in the United States of America
10 9 8 7 6 5 4 3 2 1

Elmo and Grover, Come On Over!

Originally published as *Grover, Grover, Come On Over*

123
SESAME STREET®

by Katharine Ross
illustrated by Tom Cooke

Random House 🏠 New York

"Grover, Grover,
come on over
and help me!"
called Elmo.

Grover helped Elmo.
"May I have a newspaper,
please?" asked Grover.
"Why?" asked Elmo.

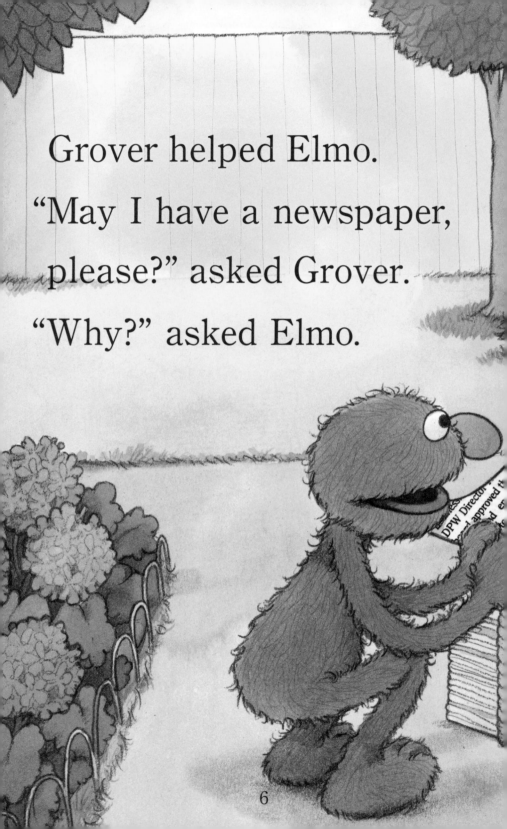

You will see!"

said Grover.

"Elmo and Grover,
come on over
and play with my kitten,"
said Betty Lou.

"Not now, Betty Lou,"
said Grover. "But may we
have some string, please?"

"Elmo and Grover,
come on over
and plant a garden,"
said Ernie.

"Not now, Ernie,"
said Grover.

"But may we have two
sticks, please?"

"Why do you need
two sticks?"
asked Ernie.

"You will see!"
said Grover.

"Do you need
my string yet?"
Betty Lou asked.

"Not yet," said Grover.

"Elmo and Grover,
   come on over," said Bert.
"Let's paint some pictures."

"Later, Bert,"
said Elmo.
"But may we use
your glue, please?"

Bert helped glue
the two sticks
to the newspaper.

"Do you need
my string yet?"
Betty Lou asked.
"Not yet," said Grover.

"Elmo and Grover,
come on over
and play at my house,"
said Herry Monster.

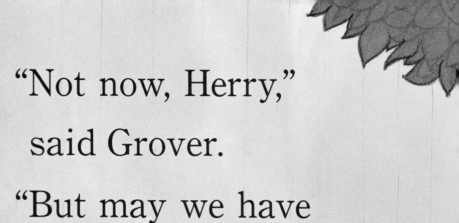

"Not now, Herry,"
said Grover.
"But may we have
some rags, please?"

"Why do you need
rags?" asked Herry.

"You will see!"
said Elmo.

Grover and Elmo
tied the rags
to the bottom
of the newspaper.

24

'Now do you need
my string?"
asked Betty Lou.
'Yes! Right now!" said Grover.

"What will you do
with the string?"
asked Betty Lou.

"You will see!" said Grover.
"Watch!"

Grover tied
Betty Lou's string
to the newspaper shape.

Everybody helped.
"Thank you, everybodee!"
said Grover.

Then all the friends
ran off to the park.
"Grover, Grover,
come on over!"
they called.

"Okay, everybodee!
HERE I COME!"
cried Grover.

We can all fly our beautiful newspaper kite!"